Adrian's Perception

Adrian's Perception

VIEWING THE WORLD THROUGH HIS EYES

Terrence Antoine

authorHOUSE®

AuthorHouse™ LLC
1663 Liberty Drive
Bloomington, IN 47403
www.authorhouse.com
Phone: 1-800-839-8640

Published by AuthorHouse 07/08/2014

ISBN: 978-1-4969-2391-2 (sc)
ISBN: 978-1-4969-2390-5 (e)

Library of Congress Control Number: 2014911787

Warning:

Before you take the time out to read this book in its entirely please be advised that minimum to no changes hasn't been made because, I wanted to keep my best friend memory alive. Please enjoy…

<u>To a love that wont exist</u>

Runners

In a state of mind

Some people run

Run to get away

And others run to find there way

They keep running until they see the light

or if it's no more light to see

Or if they are like me

They us we run non-stop with no end insight

We run non-stop because

We don't have fear no more

Not even of fear death

But just how will I or we go

What's your fear

How about you tell some one your fear

Before the fear itself keeps you running.

Boy Blue

Who's going to cry?
Cry for me, him or her, or maybe you
Little boy blue cried.
For along time
Wishing and hoping that
His all star will come back
Will you cry for little Jr. Blue?
He needs and wants to know.
Would you cry for little Jr. Blue?
While trying to commit suicide.

Would you cry for blue?
While having a nervous breakdown
Little Jr. Blue wants to know.
Would you laugh while he crying
For being taunted for being gay.
Would you cry for blue?

Blue wants to know out of all of you.
Would you cry for little boy blue?
Blue knows that you wouldn't cry for him,
But Blue will cry for you.
Because you couldn't walk a mile in little blue shoes.
I've been there and I've cried for boy blue,
but I am not crying anymore.

The truth behind little boy Blue.

Who cried for me?
Yeah me
I cried for myself when
My all star dad preferred drugs over me.
I cried when he left on Christmas eve.
Crying out while turning blue.

I cried for me while
Trying to commit suicide more than 10 times
Within a 3 year span
I cried for when it was unsuccessful
I cried because I couldn't take it anymore.

I cried while having a nervous breakdown
Because I had nothing but the Blues in me
I cried 4 years ago for being taunted because I was sexual challenged.

Now you know the truth behind me being little boy blue.
I ask the same question again now you know the
truth which one of you cried for me?
Don't be scared!
I am just telling the truth, About living in the life of me

Chapter 1

My thoughts

I do think that I did all my homework the road to redemption is hard because you have to change things and make a mends to the one that I have hurt over the course of my short filled house and that's funny to me because I am only 20 and yes I've done a lot of damage but I'm trying to do it right in 2009. I know a lot of people in the world would make these new years' resolution and never keep them, but I am going to keep mine.

The year 2008 wasn't what I would call a good year for me because my mother was still dealing with the fact that her only living and breathing son is gay. My friends was walking in and out of my life and also I realized that its time that I get back in my schedule my yellow brick road but its weird I didn't think that I would accomplish all my goals except for one I don't knock myself for it nor am I displeased but at peace cause I was able to prove to a lot of people particularly my family that I was going to leave and never come back well the never come back part may have not been true but at that time that's how I was feeling. Well I got down there and I didn't get cold turkey but set back will say. I didn't know it then but god said "O hold up what's Mr. Davis up to, I see that he accomplished just about all those goals he/we set out for him; its time more than any to throw him that curve ball". All I knew that it was like I get tripped up and sent back home with no job no money and not in school and I knew then what was going to happen depression was going to set in and I will be completely at ground zero, but my best friend Lorenzo had let an angel from god take over his body to may sure that I will not get that far on the ground but just a little before you hit the pavement with a SPLAT!! Lorenzo called and said "Get dress and get up, its no time to lay around the house but to make things happen and it did I got all my stuff to start school and that was Georgia perimeter college," it wasn't my dream college or one of my choices but hey it's a school and a whole lot cheaper that Gordon so Why not go. Lorenzo I can honestly is amazing he came threw when others felt the need to bash me and that's never good but we aren't going to go in to detail until later. I made it to the school and I missed late registration by 12 hours I wasn't mad yet again because I know he put that road block in place to get some rest of the baggage that was lingering around from 2008. Wow you guys I skipped a whole part well it was when the year flew by with drama and disappointments and a lonely night soaking in a bubble bath bringing in the new year, I know, I know pit a full I know but it was for me it was just so relaxing and I just couldn't help myself. Ok now lets skip to the now part in 2009 and how I got one less friend and how I realized that my happiness only really came from me just being by myself and the occasional moments with the friends and family that I had left in my life.

It was 9th grade year March sometime, when the graduation test was going on and I met her Monique, she and I had just met and it went from there 7 year of pure enjoyment but that not all when it got to the end it got bad and neither one of us wanted to do anything about. I don't feel like I was wrong but that we both are because we let it get so bad to it come to this. It got so bad I started not to recognize her and I went to look at these pictures that we took long ago and I remember that those was the last days when we had fun and that's said to say that the last memories that I remember the most is when she was more mad and curious about what I was doing with my life then her own and I'm mad that she couldn't see how stress that I was getting and that I felt so much responsibility on my chest that I couldn't enjoy having fun with the ones I care about. We'll this isn't meant to bash her but to just to let you guys know that it wasn't all bad just until it got to the end of it. And Yes I will miss her but its time to move on to something new. So you see it was a lot of stuff going on. Today I realized that I'm not happy, well I'm happy but not like I dream or use to dream when I was little, I was talking to all them, my friends and I was telling them that I would like to get back my roots with the family......its corny but it's the truth. I think that today I opened up a new part of myself and I'm happy that I did. With every friend that I gained I learned something new.

I wasn't sure if it was me or just some big ego trip but the truth hurts when you know it all to well, the decision to end something isn't always the best move for you or them but it in the long run it turns out to be but with me I think that its funny cause I am the one that is constantly doing the breaking up with the other person I guess that I have a 7th sense that picks up on when I know that's its not going to work and I go back to my square one. Its good to every once in awhile to step out side of your box but when you begin to step to far that's where the floor become a big thin sheet of ice and after on step it breaks. In the end I would say that each and every time that I do end something that they always tell me that they feel sorry for me but I don't feel sorry for myself because each and every guy has said the same thing to me and I know that part of its true but the other part of me know its not to feel sorry for me is to somewhat care about me and if you care then u still like me and therefore you begin to feel sorry for me because you feel as if I Adrian Davis has lost something that is so good but how can I loose something when it never really was able to keep my attention but for a spilt second and that means in my world the 2 weeks, funny huh? I guess I come to live with it, come to grips with the fact that I may not know what I want or who or why I want them but most of all I don't know another part of myself so that leads to yet another story and its getting kind of late so ill save it for a next time. My and Your thoughts are private so why are I writing it down and I want to tell the world because in that time I will have found the write one and maybe myself but till then.........

The gift of life is yes special you see that we have the ones that can and the ones that cant but still try and then find other ways to do or make the magic happen. Me, I will be put in the middle category and that the ones that can but wont get the chance to do or experience the magic that's sad to said but it became a reality to me today, now I know why I'm so in tuned with the world and the secrets that it holds and that's because I wont get to feel of experience them so in some ways I don't lack it at all but what I do wish is that I didn't feel the pain of loss so much, in a book that is now a movie called the secret life of the bee's they had a sister named may and she was born as a twin and she lost her sister she lost half of her soul, body and mind but then god gave her a gift in return she was able to feel the world and all its good and bad times but the most she every felt the most as the bad; I know how she feels she was given a gift that isn't easy nor hard to control but it just is there that's like life given It and taken it away it was a gift so why try to return it as so many women do as if they will forget the child that they aborted but some do forget it but other, others it begins to play like a song on a never ending cycle of repeat, if you are for abortion then you are yes you are a murder......... Its said that sleepless night always means that you have something on your mind other say its because of stress and others say that they just really isn't sleepy, a well all of they is correct well the simple fact is that I have done so much wrong and been so selfish that I never saw the problems around me but my own well since god has opened my eyes I have come to see the difference in between being lost and always running and since that I'm not doing neither its actually getting a little harder to stay focus on the task at hand because I'm trying to make sure that its well it's the right one but I will never know until I get down that path for a little bit but then after that you know but me I don't want to do it like that I want to trust in god that he is going to do it for me and this time since the head or my head is on straight now some what he's going to help me and make me over and put some stuff in order so I say the reason why I cant lay my eyes to rest is because that I've done enough of resting and laying around that I have to keep my eyes open to receive all that is meant for me and even though that I am tired now I seem to have enough of energy for me to do all in a days work but why cant I just let the things that stress me out let them go now instead I cant reason being that they are my burden and I have to go to the river side to lay these down to finally be free I want to be free and this time I wont forget where I came from and who I use to be so yea I know why I have sleepless nights now do you know why.!!!????!!!!… It funny all of those time when I thought that I had love it was nothing but lust and I think of all the ones that came before him they don't even matter. It was like my heart wasn't or could never be in it because my heart became as cold as the Antarctica but now some how somewhere I got on a boat making my way to the triangle in the sea only to make me fell a little weird before the big change come, the feeling is so indescribable and amazing at the same time to know that something is coming but I have to wait and relax and wait for all the rest of the other sidetrack things that might make me get off track to fly right by because I'm focused and determine to do something huge and major. I know it sounds weird coming from me the one that never know what he wants but I may still no know but I know what direction I am heading in now so I am going to stay on that one even if I have to climb a mountain during this I will so do it. I was once scared to fall for a guy or fall in love but I'm not, I want to fall in love to see if I have what it takes to be the one in love. It was a thought that I will happen in like a fairy tale but reality hit and said bitch no its not real and it wont happen like that so um try again so I did over and over on a consistence basis so let me see it was so many and they was the potential one but hey I get it now anyone can be the one but the one that can handle the ones role so there, the others wasn't the one but just the ones for in the meanwhile and that's cool cause I don't want the fake feeling I want the real one, LOVE. Carrie went in search of high fashion and love but in the process found her four friends and the call for high fashion, instead of that I stayed home and lost my since of fashion but I'm ready to be like Carrie and go in search of it but hey I look and I am a little like her but she found her love and it came to a close but then the next chapter opened but I'm a little stuck in neutral until I get over this speed bump but truth be told I might have just found my Mr. Big except the name might just be different............ or will it be.............. Ok see some one once asked me what is the big with the four letter word that we all seem to be scared of. My answer was simple, we are all scared of something new; its like when you ride a bike or skating you don't want to fail at it and some say why try something if they might at fail at it. That is a good answer but not good enough the reason for trying something and if you fail in the process is to give you the learning experience that most of us doesn't want but what we need. These become essentials in life and its hard to explain to them that this must be learned because you will always have regrets and should a, could a, would a and those are not good to have, because when you die you will have unfinished business and that interns to lead you to leave this earth with a frown instead of a smile; due to the fact you might be with the all high mighty and power full god.............................. I've so badly wanted to be part of the world outside but indeed in always stood alone and not in the spotlight until its my time, I stand out in a crowd I begin to close my eyes and stop walking and I can feel the worlds energy flowing threw my soul but yet I still cant find my spot in history or just for right now.

I had started to walk down the road and yet I still see no one but I feel a presents in the air that's following me. I continue to look behind me and I see nothing. I arrive at my destination and I see a little by sitting at the park bench; I sit next to him and I part my lips to ask him where is his parents but before the words escape my mouth he begins to talk and then let the words come out and ask me do I want to hear a story of why I sit here I said yes and he begin to tell me about all that has happened to him just before he reached the age of 7,as he tells me this it seems all to familiar but I ignore it ands let the little boy talk and he started with the Christmas from hell when he awoke to yelling and screaming from his parents bedroom and all he heard was his mother tell his father to get the hell out you don't live here anymore. He climbed out of bed and tipped toed to there bedroom and saw the sight of his dad packing and his mother stressing and crying, I look back at it now and I should have went into the room and comforted my and asked my father to stay but I see now it was for the best. What why was it for the best? The little boy begin to turn blue I jumped back he said don't be alarmed it's just from the light above me the blue light its what I like to call it. As I tilted my head I couldn't see no light then I looked back at the boy and for that split second of a mile-second he had aged no more than a year and he was the color blue still. He turned to me and said this

7

is the part of my life where I really became blue and thought that I was investable, invisible no investable, o ok I replied. So he tells me that he begin to hide from the outdoors and discover the television and other ways to express myself. I even discovered hidden talents and I've lost and no longer care that I have I also found the dark side of me the point that sleeps in the shadows of my soul. Hey everyone its been awhile since I sent a message that can touch yours or some ones life but hey here's it go, I lost a friend this year, I nearly lost my own life twice but I was saved but just to loose my mind and then once find it again, and since I've been back I cry for my happiness that I can smile laugh and enjoy life once again my head is back on str8 and I'm walking right foot left foot and is taking each day by day. My questions was answer and still is being answered and it hasn't been a day since I said I missed my old life and old ways cause I don't, I'm happy and I want all of ya'll to see that I'm new or reborn to a new Adrian Davis is no longer a failure or never was a failure but a just confused by my past had me in confinement and had me shielded fro my blessings that was meant for me but they was block now that the block is gone I see the world no longer in hate but in love. I wanted love so much that I did anything for it, I wanted attention from my family and mother and when I finally got the attention it wasn't the one wanted but the one I needed weather I choose to realize it or not it was for my better. I thought that I had found love over and over but it wasn't love cause i was thinking with the wrong head,(the one down below and not the one up top) and finally I learned that things happen for a reason and its not always when u want it to happen but trust it will come and shake the world that you know and make you a new and show u that u got a well over due reality check!!!!!!

So like it's the 1st Saturday that I'm just in the house cleaning and thinking that I am almost there to the point I got things in the right place just I haven't go the go from god and sometimes I wonder what is actually taken him so long, I know he know what's going on so why cant he just send it but them I also remember that the pastor said February is the month for me to get a job and he didn't say what part the beginning, middle, or the end so I guess its time to wait but I'm so impatient so I see why I want god to rush but if he rush this time he wont find the right job for me to stay for a while. I guess it's all in due time right lol I know so I guess I have to wait. I just so don't want to...

Isn't it funny how your life now in the present day can be destroy but a well an act of randomness and cause all kinds of confusion and chaos and you not be ready for it. Yea, I recently became a victim of this act I had anal sex unprotected I know already what you guys are saying "What the fuck made me do that to?" to answer that question truthfully I honestly don't know nope the real reason is that I thought that I could trust him like I fell to realize that trust can come over night but most of the time its not in the overnight bind at the mail room its gained now over a course of time and its become more and more rare that you can trust anyone because they, them, us as human beings has and will always have a tendency to lie cheat steal if we believe that you can get away with it. At this point I don't hate myself just disappointed that I did that in the 1st place but I'm not going to stress about it just pray to god and take the antibiotics and call it my 7 days to redemption. Also my mother told me today that a wall has fallen in my life and that it's the wall of me being gay I don't understand how one subject that we may talk about automatically goes to the topic of me being gay. So lets set the record straight I do not agree with being gay I wish and dream of one day I wont be gay but I am and more than likely I will stay this way and its unfortunate but in my case I just deal with got and embrace the lifestyle that I have I don't believe that I should flaunt it to the world so I don't it say to myself and close friends and family that I trust o, ok no lets get back on track. She doesn't realize that I didn't make this decision to be this way but I was just place in my lap and put into myself. The wall isn't due to me being gay the wall is for the wall debris on the floor was from a 7 year friend that just ended and I just don't understand how to trust or make a new wall but at this point I don't think that I need a new wall but just how to start a new structure of something new for me to enjoy and that wont be knocked down......

Today I woke up thinking or some huge changes that I have to make so what I plan to do is make them changes the problem stands in my way because I don't know if it's the right thing to do I'm Lost and confused on what to do so I think I can make it now but its going to be hard to do but Im going to make it today get ready I think this what was the lord was talking about trust in the decisions that he puts in my head. So next week I start yet another part of my soul over so im ready set go, but on another note; while I was walking in Lenox Mall today I notice and thought of something you can never really ever escape your past cause eventually all that you have done wrong it will come back to remind you of it like today when I saw two of my ex's well these two guys that I use to talk to and it was weird cause they had every good quality that a guy or girl would or do want but its like this light bulb goes on and says he's not the one so let stop this and try it again with someone new. Is that so wrong????????????

To me its becoming more and more noticeable to me its gong to be a hard task to find someone on my level and I guess of other things to, I am so lost and confused but found at the same time I'm beginning to see what people mean when they say its no one for them then you have these other people in the world telling you that its somebody for everybody ha, ha, ha, its so funny but I guess Im going to be alone for now I guess I just need to have a fuck buddy for the time being to fix this sexual tension that has been building up… or I will just might find some one just when Im really ready to give up on dead beat broke black

sorry excuse for me ......The inner thoughts are coming less and less now but it doesn't mean that I'm going to stop writing no nope not at all but in recent studies of myself I cant seem to find what I am missing so I try to find things that will keep my interest for just the ....
Today was a real good day besides running into my ex and his boyfriend I didn't feel like I should say something to him. I am happy with the person I got now its early in the stages but its has a good feeling about it I don't have doubts and I deleted my bgc and a4a account today for him and posted that me and him go out on face book its kind of weird that I did it but I feel like I can be the real me around this person the one that is happy caring and thoughtful my mind was lost and confused well still confused but I am found well I found someone that is I guess somewhat my equal... but we will see

Seeing is believing as some may say its weird because I know myself all to well and myself knows me all to well to but My best friend Lorenzo do to and to tell that he is right about something is hard to do because I feel that I am never wrong when it come to me I am always right but it's the case know I finally started to accept that yes I do have flaws and yes a lot of them but its about time I accepted them and I guess embrace them. I've crave things as any other person but I am a little bit different due to the fact that I am so head strong and when I want something I want it then and there and that need to stop now because I will continue to hurt people in this process and everyone that my paths has crossed with has shown me that I'm no longer curious about the same sex but of the opposite and that I Adrian Davis, yes I am lonely but that doesn't mean I need some one it means that I need to get to know myself a little bit more and I know I will hurt one more person but I have to do it for me, my life I s my own and I will be the one that must account for all the things that may and will go wrong and when the time of judgments I will have to answer to the lord for all of my wrong doings and at that time I will. It will be a process and a process in deed but to be straight forward I am truly looking forward to taking this journey and this time I wont be along I have friends and family there that I will take this one with and I hope that this one is better than the last trip and that it comes with stops along the way. I know that the week ahs started already but mines has just begun to change I will take charge and go for the not so normal and try different and safe things but those that of not me so to speak well not so much but what I do need is to have some good ass sex and I think its bout time that I did have some cause I want and need some at this point the sexual tension is amazing I felt my full potential yesterday and I liked it a lot but well It was always in me but hiding somewhere deep in that black hole I call a soul; now that that is not a black hole but just a light spirit and or beautiful energy that flows makes me realize that it is still hope for me and that its not to late at all ...

Lets start off by saying that I don't remember exactly when I started to run but all I know is after that day I never stopped running since then and I met people that has changed and came in and out of my life and that I am grateful to meeting them but they never could stop me from running the one person I thought could stop me did but it wasn't long enough or the pull of whatever she had on me just couldn't hold on. I know that is a problem but it's my own and I want to deal with it. My thought and saying change so much that I start not to recognize myself in the mirror on the outside appearance you would never know that I think so much and is confused and in theory to I close my eyes and just breathe to hear the wind blow and along with the bird chirping but instead I hear my inner most thoughts and worries. I've written poems and stories but they don't never seem to get finish and now that I started to complete my tasks that I start I begin to let the truth reveal itself and that my deepest secret has came out my mouth and I finally said those words Mother mom I was molested but a 30 year old woman and that's why you only son is gay and now that its said I don't know where to go I have held on to a deep dark thing like that for so long that it became my reason to excel and push forward in life and now that its out in the open I have pushing me to go forward in this manner I have the will and determination but not the desire, it's a shame that we can hold on to the negative all the time and use that to fuel us but when its all gone and when its gone you cant get it back you can never turn that positive energy or event into the fuel you need to go on. I still haven't mastered that trick and when I do ill be sure to tell the world hows its done until the mean time I think I am read to check out now for a little power nap before the rest of the day gets started, and lets see if when I dream I'm running to.

Yesterday my nephew was born Yay! me right but then I felt one sister loose one he pain and the emotion felt hurt so bad I didn't know what to do but fall down and cry but I said as I lay there on the cold pavement if its god will then it shall then be. I know me of all people to be spiritual at a time where in most confused about a lot of thing but I'm yet and don't think that it is possible to be confused about my faith in Jesus. Once again I'm back to somewhat of square one and my head is currently still being screwed back on but it jus haven't gotten tighten enough, a good friend told me that I have a lot of growing to do and he's right we'll he never stopped being right I will just not ignore him when he telling me some things. To be so truthful I didn't think that this place of confusion will or would last this long what's going on in my head? Probably they rewiring or just rebuilding some old stuff that was torn down. As each day truly goes by I start to miss a certain someone but I know it will never happen so I need to let that go, but we got so much history. I am also starting to notice that this time around I am doing a lot of things differently and that I might just be missing out on my friends. Love can come at any time so why must we wait or sit around for it tells me that huh? Its not understandable to me but Lorenzo has might has found his but I haven't found mine, I know I'm all of these things that people say my personality its true but when will someone actually try to get thru all my macho man image and see that I am a person hurt and scorn and want to fix or heal me before my body and mind do it for me…Before I conclude this little entry I wonder was selling a part of my soul was, was it really worth this torture?……The urge of wanting to run is strong but it isn't that strong anymore fighting it is real hard to do I think but my soul, well part of its still missing so that where the running comes from cause I am not whole and I and my body and mind would love to be whole. Ok so I just came back from my second date with Corey and it was fun I haven't had that much fun in along time. We understand and get each other and it not in a nasty way. This entry might be short but ill continue to write in this because I feel that is not much that I can say is that he was a complete gentlemen I have never felt so special with the hand holding the kiss on the hand and the kiss and hug goodnight. This one is different in so many way or is that I am different, did I age or just mature or how about its just the simple fact that I waited listened and grew as a person and matured in this time around well I made it to date number 3 and I cant wait for that but until then I just need to be myself and remain calm and just be happy that I have someone special like Corey. So far you guys know a lot of my inner thoughts by now but the question I want to ask is do you know what I am going to do next right, by now my inner thoughts help you understand me and some of my ways but not yet how to predict my next move. Now how bout I just tell you guy I'm going to continue to take it day by day and realize that you cant live to far in the future to where you don't enjoy the present. Now I think I want to get to planning my last date I think is it to early for me to plan nope because its not in the future, future but in the near future, yes you guys I am content, relaxed and just at a good piece of mind It make me think the wait was well worth it well damn worth it… until later today as the rest of the day unfolds o and also I didn't get the job at Comcast but hey the weeks not over yet so best wishes to me…… but one more thing I like Corey A lot he a cool dude and my friend and also my boo so far I'm not scared no more at all I'm ready to enjoy my life…. Until later, it's later and I really don't have anything to say but I got a 3rd date.

Today I said it out loud and confronted my past and I felt no ties to it, my life is at a point to where I have no complaints except that I don't have a job yet but I know I will find one but I have and be patient like I was with waiting for someone to come in my life. This song just came on and it reminded me of a friend that I lost and taught me that love can come at anytime and the lust and like can come too but if you don't know the different your really doomed to fail but I think this song reminds me of what I wanted at time and I sort of got it now so I take it I just still have to take it slow still. I close my eyes and just sit back and listen to the words and I remember all the good times that we had and how that event happened shaped me to change my life and seek a higher level of piece of mind even though its and was and still will be hard to do with people it soon to be well worth it and I see myself in a mirror smiling and laughing away cause I got that piece of mind that she had. Everything is now in its spot and now I can lay my head down and know that I have accomplished my goals and that its time to set some new ones but how about a day or 2 to wait o hold up I've never done that in the past and its not now the time to start time to make those goals and get ready to knock them out the ball park well at least my ball park in my head. Well here it goes well the 1st one is that I want to have a job 2nd get my self ready for school and take it head on 3rd Pay my bills or the people I owe off and 4th I want my friendships to stay in tack and no more drama to come up 5th I want to get my own car and 6th I want to make sure that me and Corey Go long and Strong and prevail over what's in store for me and him together and or alone. Now those are set I need to get on my grind Monday morning and next what I want to do is get some rest finally my body is crying out for some attention and its time I pay attention to it and no longer neglect it. The energy that I have been feeling is, is its something that you just must feel for yourself. The day is almost over and tomorrow is almost today and my 3rd date is here to I'm excited but I just cannot show it in person then I will be reflected every where on my face and with the body language, but I've said too much for now so you know it by now until next time...... Why is this year so different it seems as if the stars are lining up and my deepest desires are being heard its weird because I even take the time to consult the stars and they say the same thing, the gods are smiling at me for once I take it. The horoscopes are on point more than they have ever been and now all I can do is smile and think I can be really happy besides from the somewhat bad days but they wont last always and the good ones and its true when you finally push or put out good energy in the world you get it back, just try it and see and the thing that you must so is admit to the wrong doings and say that you are wrong and say I am ready to make it right so how bout ya'll do that and get back to me and see what you get, on the other side of thing yes today is Friday and its my 3rd date and after this yes I will stop counting in here but not in my head. At this point I know he's feeling me and I am feeling him to now all I can do I can do is smile when I think how happy I am and finally my love life has a little love in it and my home life is getting right and I have no complaints and I ready for change and ready to accomplish all of my goals here goes I'm up, up, up o hold up I need to keep my feet planted to the ground and not get ahead of myself so how about I just take the stair so that I can pause and take breaks before I make it to the well anticipated top of this mountain, building or whatever the hell I'm climbing this time, ok till later on tonight or the next morning details might be told wait nope Ill hold those to myself.

Chapter 2:

Its called Dating at home

So yes we care dating but not officially together and I am fine
with that I felt so safe in his arms last night I didn't even move
that's how content I was he's what I've been waiting for in the part one
of a man and he is also starting to understand me and well I know that
you guys are waiting for me to tell you what happened last night well her
it goes, we went into Ingles to get some chips and drink for the movie
and he also was high but I didn't mind that the that did bother me was
that when we walked in all eyes was on the two black guys that has just
walked in and we even had this girl follow us around the store trying to
seem as if she is investable but she wasn't I want to say something but she
was and still will be a child so who cares right. We got back to the house
he showed me around and we sat down on the floor to watch the movies
and he tell me not to laugh cause the only DVD player that works is
the SpongeBob one so he turns it on and I like flip out and start rolling
cause SpongeBob popped up on the TV screen, so we watched some of
the movie then started to make out not variously just making out calm
ands he took my breathe away 3 times and the sweetest thing ever was
that he gave the last pieces of ice so that's how I know he likes me a lot

and also what else um, um let me see we went into his room and fell asleep in each others arms and didn't move. We have a connection that is different and unique and I like that also before I go we established that we are dating and still friends lol but let me go and continue to take it day by day and imagine what I have but I cant live in the future or too far ahead so its cool now until later Piece out Today was yes a pretty good day the only problem is that yes I know that o don't have a job so why keep throwing it in my face I know, I know already that I am not contributing to the household but they act like I don't have a life of my own to live I know that I font have a job and the lack of funds stops me from doing a lot but I have friends that like and love me enough to hangout and pay for me. They my sister and my mother fail to realize that I do whatever they may say go her go there I need to be picked up from school and I need you to run and pay this bill for me and yet I don't get a thanks but just the comment, you have no job and no life all you do is sit around eat sleep and shit and that's it so why should I say thank you for you doing me a favor. Isn't it funny I know I say the same thing but yeah hey its life my life that has just started in 2009 I am for art thou there errand boy. I also confirmed that I am going to get Corey something for his birthday and take him out with what money that I do have. I also want to cry tonight because my heart is warming up inside and I feel weird I almost feel alive and free from all the sorrow I felt once before. I don't regret loosing my job but I do learn from it, I don't second guess the hand god has laid before me, I don't want to be normal I like being weird and me I like myself because I know who I am what I like and why I like it and I know where I am going in life and that no one is going to stop me so this, this shit right here will pass but I will stand or yet I think prevail is the right word for that but its getting late and church is in the morning praise him lol but goodnight you guys until tomorrow and the day starts all over once more

A certain girl told me that I was getting out of pocket and I replied girl what you talking but then I shortly realize she used it as if I was getting out of hand but instead she used the out of pocket and made it her own but the thing is when do we know we are getting out of pocket or turn or is it the line that we think is so long. When Jesus came done here and walked the streets the path ways and road became what we all know so well as a huge traffic jam instead of cars it was people and when the people of the world then did they get out of pocket yes the answer is yes lets take it when the king hung him whipped him, put a crown of thorns on his head and said here its fit for a king so later when he was hung up there what did he say to his all and mighty power father, Jesus replied God they know not what they do so forgive them of this sin and of future sins for they know not who I am, so this morning I'm going to ask you which one of you cast the 1st stone, start the 1st fight, throw the 1st blow think about it and see if you are the one truly getting out of pocket or turn and think of what Jesus did he spared us so why not spare someone who knows not of what they do for you can be the next famous person or become someone important and that goes the other way around to for all of god children a special and has a unique reason for being and living there life like they choose to live it so once I get don't get out of pocket stay inside and control yourself cause Jesus is there and even though he will forgive you don't let him do by just not doing to add to the work he has to do.

As the day slowly comes to and end I found out what was wrong with me my heart was melting it's the only logical excuse for the unexpected snow. Its was so pretty and white I know I wont see anything like that for awhile and im not sad about it at all see what was and what is not no more the warm sensation hurts at 1st but I think I can get a hold of this newly found feeling that I have so I take it but its been awhile as I see it with the lessons that Ive learned from in the past that I think that I can get a grip on the feelings that I will once again feel and fit is true so true that when you get hurt but that 1st or 2nd person that wall and the ice guns come out and start firing on your hear to protect it from any more pain that your mind and heart says it or you cannot take no more so there lets freeze it. The freeze is good for others cause they come out but for some it's the end point in there love life in my point I didn't want to let that happen to me cause I feel that I had a lot more to do than to just be alone and self driven into my career or for that matter school I know now and I have my items in order but they may not come like I want them to but I think that I can handle those task since I know what to expect from the worst from each aspect of my life so why not enjoy life until they arrive at my door step but today tonight as I sit in this house in the bathroom floor where my tub water with the stress relief is in the water I think back to all that has happen and now I see im back the real Adrian with just a hint of the new and old in the mix I smile cause it took so long and all these feelings to know that It was my inner self wanting to come forth to try this thing called life once more and now that I'm back I think I need to put some things back in order and I guess enjoy and celebrate that the real me is back now that the heart is truly back on I don't know what to expect but for the record the backbone is still here so step if you think I will but up with your bullshit as I so call it but everyone my tub is calling my name and its cold on this floor to but tomorrow is the 4th date and his birthday so yeah it's a big day so wish me luck until tomorrow u know …

You know when the president address the nation I address my future readers its another day in the house except its Monday morning and the family is here it hasn't been that easy since they got the day off but I am dealing with it but listening to my music well I did the counting to and its been 3 weeks almost a month that I have been talking to Corey that great news I also decided that its time to delete some of my past and that includes the last email that ties me to the past this one last thing. In other topics I got the perfect outfit for my date tonight and Corey has started the checking in thing and its cool I like that he don't feel obligated but he just does it to make me smile to know that I still got him and he got me, I think that I am coming to the attachment stage but I'm a little uncertain that I'm there yet or not but as it progresses ill find out what is really up. On the sadder things of life I well its been the 3 night that I have had the dreams about death and I guess since I sold my soul when I was so little I didn't know what I was doing and now that the part that sold my soul is back with a new soul I think that the demon or devil wants to kill this one, so he is attacking me thru the subconscious mind or is it that I'm making it up...

Yesterday wasn't really nothing to report except me and Corey decided to cancel the date because he got off late and I knew he was tired but the good thing is that we are on for tomorrow but today I put a lot of stuff and I begun on my grind even harder than I ever today, reality hit me hard and I fell and hit that pavement before the money really went out. I understand a lot about myself and I'm scared because my truth tend to hurt the ones I love but this time it might be different because this time my heart is not ice cold but warm as a fresh spring day getting ready to change into a hot summer day so there its nothing really to it, I shouldn't be afraid of the unexpected but just ready to tackle it and say I'm no longer scared of what to come, ha that's funny, not. Today I also found time for myself even though I was with friends it didn't matter I was in my own world so that the outside influences shouldn't matter at all I just should be free to do me and still take day by day somewhat lol well goodnight its wasn't nothing really special about today at all......

Once again I find myself writing about the experiences that I have its funny cause I'm starting not to have write so much in here because it becoming more and more normal something that I am starting to like so much I didn't think that I can do it but I will by the grace of god and the trust in friends myself and him. Well I gave him a taste of what I can offer him and of course he wanted more but he wasn't going to get it but its cool, he held me and its like we are together but not, I hope that you get what I am saying if you don't then later you will he checks in with me apologized for doing something wrong and I am starting to fell weird I think this is what falling for a certain someone now but hey I am happy that it is him the attention and affection says it all he got me at a 90 degree angle can he get me to the 360 to prove that I really do like him.

Well I am done for now cause I need to take my nap lol but no you guys its just that he gets me I get him and he get me and we talk and workout problems than going outside the source all the time he is what I want ….but I also want a job and money and me to be in school to so you tell me what to do, I already know but do you?

Ok I know this entry before this one is a little weird well a lot of weirdness going on, so in this one I get back to the normal well this one just will be strictly updates on everyone that in my small but big little world I call my head.

Tamia—well she doing good, her secrets are still is the most well know female in morrow high school he mouth has gotten smarter than ever but it wouldn't be her if that mouth wasn't born and matured a lot.

Lisa- well we are back on somewhat good terms I don't know how long it will last but I hope for awhile because I really do miss my sister.

Keisha- um what to say she got her hands full with her family the new baby and the baby daddy but most of all she is trying to loose that weight, the baby weight.

Sharon-My mother- she is still her she changed a little and matured but you know she's forever changing so well just waiting for the next thing.

Me- I'm happy at home school coming up I'm still looking for a job and my love life is great what more can I ask for.

Corey —well he's mine that's it no its not he my friend and now special friend and now we are dating and he is going to meet mommy soon.

Ok well the update is cool in all but I guess my life is really getting on track so I am like in super weird mode I don't know what to do anymore day by day is worked and I'm not finding my life less interesting than I thought my tears are dried up and my emotions are back I've forgiven all that has hurt or left me in my life and I am on the straight and narrow I take it but also what I've learned is that it is my season and I just got the over flow so now I either can wait for it of go out and find it but what I decided to do is do a 50/50 thing to see what I get and also praying to may help well it will help. Today I decided that my life is interesting but not to me anymore the events that take place in my life will come and go but it will be me. In the mean time I will write down the interesting plots or events that happen in that day and it will have the dates too on them so I can remember them…….until whenever…

(March7 2009) To me yesterday was the day lesson that we learned was patience and yes we learned it after like the 3rd place we went to but I guess its cool I had fun well the date went well we went to the movies dinner and I drove his car and on a positive note I met his friends and they like me and they are pretty cool o and I gave him a surprise after the date was over he liked it cause he rated me a 10 on that one and a overall process its weird because before I think it he does it and or finish it. On a bad note his ex-friend called but he blew them off 6 to 7 times but like I said one bad thing doesn't get to me on a good note I enjoyed myself and I am starting to like him a lot...

The question I asked today if its my season then why doesn't it feel like it the negative energy still try's over and over till I give in nah I cant and wont do that I begin to feel my fingers on the piano and I just cant seem to bring myself to play the song in my head. My mother went off today well tonight and she said I am not the real definition of what a boy is and that I'm selfish and ungrateful and that I belong on the streets but the truth is that I don't care anymore cause she don't affect me no more her word don't matter unless they are meant to help me instead of destroying me and my spirit and also truth be told I really don't care if she meet Corey cause I will not put up with her bullshit anymore and I will no the embarrassed by her no more I am my own person and that what counts she don't and cant see me as her son because of what I am but like I said I don't care I will make it with her or without her there. Well din her defense I guess I can make one wish for her I want to be a real boy naw fuck that I am one just not the one she wants me to be......

(March 10, 2009) Today was a pretty easy day my allergies went like a little crazy but I took two pills and went out to sleep so yeah well my play brother Devin came home today and we went o go see Tee and her new dog called beauty; she cute by the way and she's a read noses pit. Devin and Tamiais playing card and me I just needed to write after today I realized that yes I might just might be sprung and that is a good and a bad thing the good is that I realized that I like him that much but the bad thing is that he is able to hurt me but its part of life that hurt comes. On the same subject I miss him now he hasn't called or texted since earlier but its cool ill wait until I get that call or text but until then I'm going to say peace out for today cause shit happen to day that was really worth writing or typing about.

(Sunday March 15, 2009)-Its been awhile since I have wrote on here and since I have empty's my thoughts but is ok I guess I figured out how to make life work but the most recent thing is that I guess you can say my time is coming and it's a little weird so this is how it feels when you know your about to die but not know when or how but the final signs or sign has come my great Aunt came to visit my mother last night in her dream to I guess to brace herself but the vision wasn't of me but of her so that's how I know that she meant me my mothers son. I want to cry but I cant all my tears are finally dried up and that now that my list is finally coming to and end I guess I can say that I am happy satisfied and content that he can take me now I wont be mad or sad I will just say happy cause I will finally be at peace but the only thing is that why is he going to take me after so much that I want to do and accomplished and now that I finally have my head on right he wants to snatch me up ha ah ha, I laugh cause you will never know the real reason just know its your time, but on the bright side of things yes family friends and life is going good me and Corey had a little bit of some problems but its ok cause we working threw it now and even though I am scared to see the out come but instead or walking away from it I am walking to it and I cant wait to see the outcome some what but in my heart and mind I know that I can accomplish what I want to so with him and that is to talk to him and to be with him I know it's a lot to ask but I want to ask it now better yet god said claim what you want and I am doing that but I really have to get ready for church so um yeah bye.

Well in recent news me and Corey is over its funny because I thought that he was mature but I was wrong but on the other had I knew that he wasn't the one for me but its was nice to have in the mean time as some may put it. I told myself this will be different and that I will make it in life and yet it feels like I am standing still but in reality I'm not. The events are taking place and its moving slowly but surely. Tonight she made the 1st move on what the family and I call the break down process to where when my mother comes into contact with something she doesn't like she will destroy it. I cried cause I remember the all the pain she caused me with all the confusion she loves so much.

These last few day has been hell on wheels and my masks has been staying on but just doing a lot of switching more that normal. The pastor told me that my life wont get any better cause I wont forgive my father but to me I have forgave him and let it go but I guess that god told him to tell me because times running out and I might miss what he want to give me but the question is how do I do that If I believe that it cannot be done, like I use to say all is reveled in due time and it different cause it nobody else's life but my own. I want so much and in so little time.

How do some of us take the truth my truth is always seem to be entering threw my door even if I don't want to hear it, and that because my message of the truth comes from up above to show me that I cant do it the way I want but I must do it by the way its suppose to be or how god has set it to be, I finally want to cry cause my truth and my past has caught up to me so now what should I do, o I know the answer and it is that of so many would agree with I need to finally let it all out but I, me Adrian Davis is scared cause im afraid of the pain that I hid so well, the question I ask will it take me out we will see......

Days and weeks has past to equal a month and I found some more clarity in my life and I came to grips with a lot more that I intended to come to terms with but its ok now I may not have all that I want but I do have my peace of mind now and that is what matters the most. I am the same person but with a different outlook on life and that's cool with me I find that with so many different out looks I can understand a great many of different people and that the neat thing about that well to be honest I have been feeling a little sick every now and again but im dealing with it now and the dizzy spells are getting a lot worse and even though my water intake has increased they seem to not decrease. I find myself wanting to cry but cant and when I cant it begins to rain out side and when my heart felt like it was warming up again it began to snow lightly and when I feel confused and lost I begin to wall and stand and see that the wind blows constantly and hasn't decided which way to blow because my sense of direction is gone. I find myself becoming more in tuned with my surroundings ......in the end I don't have anymore changing to do until the next time that I feel the need to evolve lol but until the thought s build up again but fyi something interesting is in the making coming soon......

Chapter 3

The bitch has checked out and Adrian is back in the hisouse!

It's a little weird cause the bitch well she's gone just yesterday I felt nothing but now I feel, I feel everything that's going on and I guess that its bout time to tell you guys what has happen since I haven't been writing in here in awhile. So you guessed it my love life sucks like hell so that I decided to be like randy and wait for it to come here to me at my door step. Its only one small problem this thing that I think I like Darius we never really ended we just stopped and that my unfinished business is back but once again I have to put it on hold cause its my time and now that school I starting back up again and I got a summer job and I applied for section 8 and will soon apply for food stamps to make it on my own its time for me to go. Last Sunday ms Maddie opened my eyes and told me what god wants me to do an im doing it now I am scared but I will do it finally to prove that im not a failure or the bastard baby she thinks I am. Now back to me some new changes are coming and its bout time I get back to telling you guys bout what's going. I didn't think that it could happen but I is, I will start the elimination process all over and its said to see that one of my good friends is bout to go in there.

So school Is about to start and im not nervous no more but happy that I completed yet another one of my goals list and for that I am great full and is once again to make a new one but I have to think about something that I seem to still have a problem with and that is love, so say once you give up that when you find it but in my case I Adrian isn't giving up on it yet just taking a break cause its time for me and what I can do for myself I am once again back on the straight and narrow and is bout to establish myself and who I am in the world. So you guessed it new journeys is bout to come up especially when we go to new York o god get ready but until then since ive checked back in ive done a lot of stuff to prepare for the future I just have to wait for the outcome and Im ready but waiting patiently I can no longer close my eyes and dream bout the things I need to get finished I can open then and see them about to unfold before my eyes and feel the ground tremble cause the devil is getting pissed and asked me how is that I am living when I sold my sold my soul to him and I replied god saw me struggling to make my own decisions and said he, well I must learn and once I started to remember who I am he asked me what do you want and I said my soul the answer was given I can not give what was taken by the devil but how bout I restore your faith by giving you a new soul of your own and of no one else the soul you giveth away wasn't your but yours and many but now I give you your own cause you have earn it after all the trouble you went threw to get here. Later the devil replied but he cant give you that back and I said did you not hear me, he gave me a new one all my own and yes its not tainted by you or the world but one that is brand new. He disappeared and then reappeared and said you want to make a deal and I said I done making deals with you so in his face I said the Holy Spirit has my back god will help me when I am down and Jesus will protect me from you. Since that little sit down he has tried over and over but not yet once has I gave in cause why would I want to leave this new world that im building from the grown up. I have some old friends and a few new ones and I finally have let the search for finding love go but let the love of my life find me because that's when the real magic will happen. Also today I felt how god is going to take me out of here and it wont be pleasant but of what I expected......what is it ....but that time isn't here yet so why not speed up the pace and get these new dreams out my way and here's the new list

> Get my 21 credits to transfer
> Get a job
> Save for a car
> Move Out
> find a school to transfer to.
> well Tba

These past few weeks so much was changed thanks to me I feel so accomplished in my new life that I have a sure fix on I have a car a job well maybe 2 jobs and im working to become bigger and better but with every new deal it came a cost in some ways was a relationship, a friendship, and me finally stand up to my mother and tell her what needed to be said. I've learned that so much can be changed by you as person take control of the sail boat and steer it yourself, the obstacles that get in your way are meant to be knocked down I wanted so much for myself that I even fabricated a fantasy world that was never meant to be but I tried to make it work but it didn't in the end cause I was trying to deal or make something last that was never meant to. I had to learn in these few short weeks that something are just not meant to be so why try so hard to keep it but just finally I need to let it go. Me as an individual constantly changes and for that I am grateful that god had given me a chance well a second chance to make me do it like it was meant for me to do it, and to think that I felt lost and incomplete and what I was missing was myself in the equation and now that I'm in the right shoes and on the track I will begin to run a new a journey with no where or end in sight. Certain stop that I made along the old road wasn't for me but for the bitch in me, I have never felt so much alive in my life and now Its time for school, career, life and most importantly My love life just wait Yeah I know I said that I was thru with love but Love to be honest isn't done with me...............Time will tell what life has for me now that I hit the reset button and well Im off to bed because Yeah I got class tomorrow morning at 8am lmao yeah 8am ......

So I went to class and by the end of the day I had added two classes then dropped to and ended up with only two classes to take, don't ask how I manage to do that but I just did, Those kids that go there has no since of style and in my opinion no direction to what they want to do in there life and then you have us transfer students and transit, o and also the adults who is there to get and education and get out there to transfer and get our degree. Well the latest of my love life I still haven't fallen for no one yet and Its weird I know that I am getting closer to the one I am ment to be with but they are still far away but its cool I just don't know what to say or do anymore but now that I am back In play mode and that my stuff is together I am free and ready to soar. I am no longer trapped in a 16 year old body but now brought to the future and set in my 20 year old body and I feel so much better because I, I got all that I want to get and know I will keep going and stride to do my best not to get side tracked and or fail because that is no longer in my mouth. To get back to the roots that you set so long ago is hard but you set them early to know when the time come you can come back and take charge again. Today I have to go and take that drug test and then where ever that mother needs to go before she goes out well to work. In other news In my love life summer of 2009 Duron wants to take me out to the movies today but I don't know if he is going to come so ill keep u posted but me and him talked for awhile last and I enjoyed him and he enjoyed me and I also learned another lesson, not yesterday but a min ago, my love life is my own and If I feel then need to share it with you, you can have opinions but that what they are just your opinions cause my decisions shouldn't be based on your opinions …well that's it for the morning let me get threw this day now.

Well as we know the date fell threw lol but its cool, I found a way to do school and work but one thing just went wrong the car I have to buy a replacement hood for the car but its cool I asked Monique for the money and she said it was cool and I can get it from here the other stuff become vital now well I started my new job at sears and the 1st day I got a number well the way I got the number was a little tricky but its ok we started talking.

To tell a story you would have to be the one that learned the lesson but in this particular story I decided to not be that person but the one that learns from the outside world and actually learn the lesson and say that I don't want it. This time I've planned to do it big well in the as jasmine Sullivan said dream big if I want to do this right in order to get it right.

Its so much in my mind that wants to come out and be said but I don't think it will come and my sexual frustration is at a all time high and I don't know why I want to run and hid but I cant, I dare to dream big but it s not way I can because it quickly get deflated and I become consumed with rage and anger and want out but it just seem like its no way out from a never ending pain. Today was a different day filled with all of emotions and kinds of stuff and its due to the face that I finally has given Lee away he got my approval last night and now that I don't need to really need to help him but help myself and I started today because I didn't realize how much I like and that I'm falling for JT my baby Its only him and Wasn't I the one that said that I wasn't going to fall for anyone anymore… more to come just wait

Well truth I thought about it I was in strong like and nothing more but after this week a lot has changed and some tigers has finally decided to show there true strips its confusing to think that this trip that we so long anticipated had become know as the trip from hell as this airplane ride back home to Georgia I can say that I finally know a new part of me but lets get back on track its not even funny how much pain and suffering came from someone that we should call family, yes I get that she's my sister but as now I want nothing to do with her she destroyed what happiness that we have found so much from ones mouth stuff was said that was bound to come out I feel sorry but then again I don't because did it to herself and by her own will. I see that blood sometimes isn't thicker than water due to the face that someone I call sister isn't my blood knows more bout me then you ever do oe will ever know. Old people once said that you can be unfinished wood and the ones that talk bout you is the sand paper and they can rub and hit and abuse u and use you but yet you will come out all nice an finished and there they sit and stand all alone. Its funny what is about to go down this is a battlefield and this war wont be won by just by strength alone but by thinking and finally cornering a cat well this particular cat In the corner and finally bring everything to the light cause its long overdue we was once scared to dance with her but we figure instead of going in as on go in as a team and do some damage beware the wonder twins is here and ready to take you down

Wars has came and gone but the truth was thought to had be passed down through the generations but the truth cannot be always true due to the face not everyone can tell the truth well the real truth but the truth of there own remembrance it becomes comical cause we take it as the literal truth and its not. This summer has truly captivated me and shaped me a little more the truth be knowing that some stuff is left to be secret and not told and I have a few but the things is that there mines and will stay in my head until I feel the need to tell my truth. Once again I close my eyes and dream bout a life inside of a world that will never exist for me, I am no longer mad at it but I just laugh due to the fact that its my life and I am in control and got a good head on cause I can say that the next time in enter in the storm I will bring me and umbrella cause I need something to shield me from something's that want to harm me until I guess next time well its just one thing I'm going to leave you with a riddle ___----___----in my past I've had fun at Atlantic station even a little drink of his tea -----so who am I Talking about well I once loved and a was loved back but I had to mess it up but not no more I will continue to fight for what I want and he might just be the one I want or not but as I say now Time will tell and if not there is others but maybe not for me until I am ready so the last questions I begin to ask myself is Am I doing the right thing? do I like getting hurt? Will I truly find love and most of all Is the things that is unfinished should I finish them?

Last night you guy I did go out and had a good time and I look good older and acted more mature and the feeling was good. I didn't remember how much fun that I had with him but I did and most of he came and was on time that what got me I can actually got some thinking to do cause that bring the total up to five and its now to work my magic and see what can happen while staying on track but one thing is clear the truth isn't always good nor bad its just the truth and it either set you free or knock you back in my case it set both of us free. The competition for my heart has begun and we will see who will last to the end...... o and one more thing this was one thing that was left unfinished in my case I needed to reopen this case to fully see where it could go.

The summer is slowly coming to a close and it seems as if everyday life is about to take place and I start to think will this year be any different since Tamia is graduating and Im back in school and my mother is thinking bout going back to school and is it that she also wants to go back to school only time will tell but until then I guess Ill have to wait. And also it comes to when I begin to prepare for the end and this plan I made to take effect and I seem to close my eyes and want to cry but I cant because its truly nothing to cry about and I finished all of my past ties and to think I am ready for the real stuff with a certain someone named Jamal, its been almost 2 month next week that him and I have been talking and the twist is that he's my sexual chocolate man and nothing more or less and I find myself falling for him more and more and it's a good thing cause I know where my emotions are and I know that they are real for him and nothing that is unfinished but on a down side of things I seem to be starting to feel like Me and my best friend Lee is just about to the end of our friendship rope and I start to think where is the real best friend that I can go to the end of time with cause I am starting to feel Alienated and I want to scream and Tell him the truth but something says wait and I will until the time is right. As of today plan one is in effect and im taking my solo rode and I am ready for this trip alone cause its bout time but also one thing is becoming true to me that I will fall in love sooner than I think. Until later

Chapter 4

Changing Tires on my Car(s)

When it comes to cars need to take care of it whether you want to or not so here goes this chapter was inspired by my best friend Lee Its how I managed to take care of my many cars that I seem to have now so the title named Change tires on my car(s). Well see when say tires I really mean changing out the guys that just don't seem to fit into what I call my dream car well dude but some parts seem to be missing so I just end to pull the part from another car or tend to program it into the car so that I will have it. Well you see I have a lot of cars that I'm taking into consideration, its just about like 3 well truly 4 it could be a possible 5th car but that one just seem to unwilling to change the color of his car and get his gear in drive. But the others are *Jamal, Bryson, Juan, John and Darius*

Each of these guys has most of what I want but then it comes down to which guy can handle the full package that comes along with me and being my new car so now comes the description of the guy and what cars they match up to.

*When it comes to **John** he's that car that you don't want to let go but you know u need to cause you are tire of putting so much time and effort* and more so money into it you start to wonder is he worth all that u put into cause you still cant get that car to run a month to where you don't have no more problems out of it and now I get to thinking I will compare him to my dodge intrepid the year 2002 where that was the worst year to get that particular car its sad to say but in all honesty I still have feelings for him and they aren't weak and that what makes its so hard to let him go cause I want to know what can be but then I start to imagine and it just not might be what I'm thinking that it will be. I can Finally say that this particular car gone due to it not passing it emissions test its funny how you can see you life with you riding with them but when it don't pass that's when your done with that particular car and its time for a new one and or how about I just pick on of the other ones to drive well it came to an end shortly after I made up my mind that this car wasn't never really for me at all just a show car with no horse power.........

The expression even though it glitters and shines baby it just isn't gold but fools gold it looks like but never is, this brings me to **_Bryson_** he's new but its weird he has a good conversation, and he continues to make me laugh and smile and had become a regular and so far its all shinning but o I just done know if that's the right way to go to get the car that you need to fix up and make it yours and etc u know what I mean laughing out loud. I as can a car have friends the answer is no but when you ask can your car become a friends car the answer is yes and that's just what this car has become a friend or a c are left in the dust said to say so much potential but it never knew when to stop and think and to say lets go in another gear and that's why he, well it the car is still sitting there in the dust or well you know where in the junk yard for recycling. Sorry but it wasn't meant to be for me to drive you just to test drive. I didn't leave this car alone just turned it into a rental car.

Then when it comes to **_Jamal_** I don't know what to say its so weird cause I can see myself with him and set for life with no worries or care in the word cause I would know that I have him and he with m. To be honest

I start to question it then I begin to say that my inner most feelings is what I want and the what I want to portray to the world is something else, is portraying an image that isn't true what I need to do or to be true to myself and then I go back to my Jamal and all the car that I have liked rode in and just wanted only one come to mind and that is my great grandfathers Red Lincoln that just captivated me ever since I was a younger kid but this car just seem to more than a car because I look at my Great Grand parents and I see all that they have been through they are still together and going strong and I go back to thinking that I want that I really do but then I get back to that image and it wont been seen as much but as something different but in my case I can be something special like I want in closing only time will tell I seem to be waiting on time cause time yet waits for no one. Time only tells me that In time I will fond love no matter what. So when I think about Jamal I see that green Lincoln that still has me today just like he do, he might just be that one I fall in love with no matter what......Will or wont I say to death do us part? Some cars can be sitting in the drive way with no particular usage at that point in time and that what is going on with this I don't know where to drive this car cause I don't turn or is it because I do turn to many heads and that the car don't make me feel the way it use to make me feel when I 1ˢᵗ got it and I know things get old but d don't get old if you are just renting instead of making payments to keep It. I start to think what to do or to say because I'm stuck in neutral with this particular car and I just can't seem to move it why is this? and I start to climb out the car and test drive other ones but its still there so I'm like what is really wrong with me and I know test driving them is wrong but I say hell the cars in the shop so I might as well but I know its so wrong but them again its not my car I'm like damn what to do ugh!!

The mind became made up and time took it place and I came to the conclusion that yes it had all the stuff I wanted but I just didn't have me in the driver seat taking it off the lot.

I learned from this lesson is that you can look pick and choose what you want in a car but the things you put in isn't what you wanted. You can fix and old car up but it still will end up with the same old tricks!!!!!!!

Some of us start out making a list and daydreaming about the man or the female that we want of our dreams down to the T. to be honest that's where we fall short of that inch of a mile, we try so hard to make some one something that they are not and in the end you are the only one that ends up sad and alone watching the movie waiting to exhale. Then on the other hand you have us other ones that start over and start to rethink us as a person and start to search for something or someone we forgot along the way and it was you.

Chapter 5:

Digging for me = A new beginning

I use to think that the place I went to escape it all was in my head.
I use to believe that everything happens for a reason.
I use to believe that life was fair.
I thought if I was good, good things would come to me
I thought if you kept your faith strong u can make it
I use to have a dad, and a great aunt
I use to think that they would return to me
But all I see is just plain ole me
I use to believe in myself and now all I have is self and the pity I sit in
As I hold on tight as the train come to a stop
and the train conductor announces
"Misery City"
I know that I've arrived
This trip wasn't one I thought I would take again
But I have
This trip is meant for me to come back
But I won't
This trip was suppose to open my eyes
But they're closed
The trips I use to take had roundtrip written on it and now all it has is
One way
I step out the train and open my eyes as I clutch
my bad tighter I see nothing but one light

That leads to the stairs
I begin to make my way up and I feel it
It is the darkness, emptiness, loneliness, and the fear but most
The tear that I cry is so black here its looks like
a women's mascara running off my eyes
I close my eyes and start to think how I got
to this place and them I remember.
I always felt unsatisfied, unwanted, not needed, and
hated on, but most I all I felt as if I didn't belong.
Those countless nights that I tried to take my life no one was
there the overdose I repeated and then there was the cutting
my wrist and so much more left me with nothing but despair,
and today of all day I felt something else I felt my desire,
willingness to live slip away and it wasn't until I realized that
I lost my soul and I cant seem to see where it went and not I
sit in this last spot alone cold and wet crying tears of black.
And as I feel the air begin to get thin I say one last rhyme
Out of sight
Out of might
I see and fear you no more
Go away your lingering endless night
I will not give up my fight
You took so much
And now it my turn to take it back
You endless night go and I wont say please
Just leave might sight
Cause u cannot have this child
For you are not my father but
The evil within
So go now; leave me be for I came and now you and I shall leave
this place I use to call Home sweet home "misery stop 101"
Now you my place and my struggle with no secrets or lies told
My soul is old but my heart is new but all old tricks boo.
So much was said so much was told but will you see or tell that
1 that she can stop because she can't hurt me no more.
You see I took her words for granted but now
I just ignore and put you on mute
For this is the last time I will tell you
I still have my hope.

Ok so fall semester has come and yes I'm back in school well where I left off at I went in to this semester with be being on academic probation so I decided to be smart and well take two classes only to get off probation. Well since then I've meet and talked to my cousin I never knew I had me and my dad is doing pretty good and home is home. I have been out of work for 3 weeks now and I have three ways to try and get a job well because I got a lot to do. I have thought about it and I said that I will take this year out with a boom, boom POW so um yeah. I think about a lot of what I been though and I've been making it have but on the bright side of things I found a new friend and I wasn't looking for one but just looking for myself. Ok I Started to see that I became a different person since the summer events and other stuff that has tool place. I lost and gained new friends and found those old ones that kept me grounded and that really did car about me. Once again it brings me to feel as if I didn't pick the right field of what I want to do in my life and for career wise. I have come to a cross roads and my soul is crying out and the person that I buried so low in my grave yard is knocking and knocking hard, because he wants out of this; well wants out of that box I put him into. I start to think back to see why I put him in the ground, 6 feet under and as of now he had started to breathe again I want to sig to save him but then I ask myself is it logical or reasonable to do and make such a hasty decision. Some people never let there heart be heard they shut it down and just step in to the real world with a real job or what society has made us to think that it's a real job. Should I cry? No not all because I'm not a mistake my life isn't a mistake but a blessing from the lord to show me and tell me that I can do the unthinkable and that's to follow my true dreams. Now back to the other subject I met someone that makes me smile and want me for me and what I can do for him; in time more will come about this special new person in my life that has started to warm my heart and I want to take this chance to actually fall in love and I shouldn't be so cold hearted but more step better but to become warm blooded again. Get ready for the adventure that I will shape and that will bring in 2010 and take 2009 out with a boom, boom POW!

In the past we've talked about a lot about family, friends, past lovers but never really on the subject about my self and my over all feeling about what going on or the situation at hand where and what happened to the real me?

I use to say that I lost myself but, I don't think that I lost myself I just blocked him out of my mind because I started to think that me the old me was in adequate to make it in this cruel world but I came to this conclusion that I want myself back because I miss me the real me that u buried underground. I close my eyes and see the spot that I buried myself in this dark damp place that looked to had been abandon but someone famous, I walk around the house; the side of the house I see broken windows and some that is boarded up but most of all, what I see on the other side when I turn around is a flower garden that is flourishing and is so amazing. In all the in chaos beauty is still sustained. I begin to walk closer and suddenly I hear a voice call me from the house, I run and knock down the a door that you can tell that was so nice but it barely hanging on by its hinges, as I ran in I fell to the floor and the voice got louder as I got inside and I become amazed by the architecture was just spectacular but once again I remember that I wasn't there to notice the art work and then I started to creep up stairs and look in the rooms to find that voice that is calling my name, as I turn the corner and see that as if this part of the house was just frozen in time cause nothing was messed up but sustain, the voice became louder and then I said come in and sat in the chair looking out the window is my great aunt and I begin to feel the burn sensation right the tears start to run down my face and I run to her and I just cant stop cry and she hands me a tissue and say wipe your face we don't have much time left this dream is almost over, I get one chance to help you and I am; so I begin to listen to her. I begin to look at the walls and the paint and wall paper begins to fall and fade and I ask what's going on and she replies time is no standing still and the last things she tells me that this is all and can be yours, you just need to dig yourself up and take back what u tried to hide I know what you have become and I am not disappointed but proud of you in what or whatever you are you are my cookie monster and nothing can change that so what I need you to do is run back out side before the house falls and save yourself from having this broken dream your dreams mean a lot and I want to see you reach them from the sky above and I know that don't start crying use that pain and anger and desire and you dig and dig down deep below to save that little boy that you was so scared that he was not capable of being in this world and its not true you do matter you and him are and is meant to be one person you guys matter and most of all remember that I love you truly I do. I close my eyes and begin to feel the tears to fall down and I get up and run, run as far as I can to get to the outside before the house falls and the dream is canceled out once more stopped but the life choices and the way things happen for a reason. I barely make it with seconds to spare. The coffin door open and out pops me and then this light come around me; well in a since us and all I can feel is so much love no more hate or confusion but the power of knowing I can make it and as I ascend or we ascend to the sky the house begins to repair itself and the light gets brighter I feel me and him coming closer and closer together and then as we become one I awaken from the dream, not scared but in a since I feel whole, and in the dark I sit crying my tears of joy to know that she saved me and has and will continue to watch over her Cookie monster. That dream plays over and over in my head knowing that I got a second chance, I am not making a mistake to become a teacher or in being gay and or more so in feeling like I don't matter I am just fine and as this semester will come to an end you will see that my dreams and my new but old life is just beginning.

What is it that drives us or in my case to be better and go above and beyond the goals that has been set with the limitations that we call dreams? I have had so many in so little of a time frame but some, yes I say some have been achieved but so many I've haven't lived up to. When starting over or when getting back to your roots is it essential to set goals or try to achieve the one that wasn't completed? The answer to myself is quite simple you do both and you try and bend over backwards to do what must be so in terms I will achieve success with getting my 30 credits to transfer to get a job the I will stay at have good grades a high grade point average get in touch with myself and with the family I still seem run away from but most of all have a good and everlasting serious relationship, o but like the minor stuff like take my defensive driving class and o yea get my license back to be mobile again to get a car that is my own and try to pay off my debuts um yeah you see I said try. The day I realized that I was being held back was the day the lady in the church told me "its time you can let them 3 go cause they not helping you go forward but just in neutral, don't be afraid to make your way to the front seat and go in drive," metaphorically speaking.

As I lay in my bed getting ready to watch The Wendy Williams Show I begin to reflect on this particular day because I finished my book well the 1st one and as of now I am on the second one I know stop gloating, because I don't even know it the 1st one will be on the bestsellers list but I am hoping that it will be on that list. I want so much to happen but I can only wait I seem to be on the right path but as of now I'm still missing one thing and I don't know what it is because I a new best friend family got my back and a new love School and actively looking for a new job so what else could I want. The answer is I'm missing my heart and inside that heart is the one thing I fear is Love.

Chapter 6:

Train Carts of a dream

I ask myself
Do I exist or am I just there?
I've come so far but yet its still a challenge
My shoes are all worn and torn
My feet hurts from running so much
My eyes burn because I've cried so much
The thoughts, they try to come back over and over
And I call but this time no one answered
No one hears me no one can see the silent tears
No one can hear my the inner my crying out
Screaming to the top of my lungs asking
Begging, pleading for help
But no one comes
I go and run in to the room
That room
Another room trying to escaped
Get away and yet it keeps coming for me
It never ends
It tells me that I can get out
I don't have to feel like this
I don't have to live like this
But most of all it hears me
My cry for help

And its just one thing after this is all said and done
That I wont be heard no more at all
Cause the number 6 will go in to place and the
Dark is what I will only know
Silence stiff
Without life inside of me I lay
Content relaxed UN heard but finally heard
And all it took was for me to take my own life
And to be lowered six feet under
And now they sit and cry
Scream hoop and holler
But for what you never heard me crying for help
So stop crying and deal like I did not being heard
So I Took a knife the sharpest one I can find went into the bathroom
Turned the light out
Fell to the floor
Cried silently in the bathroom thinking is this the best move
And I hold the knife in my right hand
And I jab it in my chest with my last bit of life
All I could do is cry
Because they didn't ever know

Late night are so very rare to be considering that I go to be bed at 10 pm but this particularly night was a Friday night and I just could not get to sleep at all so I decided to do the one thing that most people my age would do and that facebook and or MySpace but in my case it was neither one but the other space which Is called bgclive.com. This website focuses on the gay community so yea you can imagine what I was doing. I was email all of the cuties on there but then I came across James's page and I hit him up, but thinking that he wasn't going to email me back and then the minute before I was about to log off the website and we have been talk ever since then that Friday night that's the day that I found him hmmm on the 21st. I can admit I was bored and I didn't think that I would go this far but it has I feel compelled to tell him the truth and not lie I miss him but most of all we well our relationship is the only one that feels like it can work and it will work. I wasn't looking for anyone; just for someone to talk to that night and I got that and so much more and it has went from there and age difference but I don't care because you help the one you like and hopefully he will be the one I can fall in love with one day but until then my dating life is going to go good and I truly count down the day that I see him.

This train ride is so bumpy and I just can't seem to lay my eyes to rest without being woken up. This is the last trip back and the closer I get back to the real world I find myself regaining my color back and my eyes and clothes also is drying as well. I can't help to wonder what brought me back on this train and almost on a non returnable ticket to. I didn't have to think so hard because I know and it's sad to say it my mother; she manages to push a button in me that just want to go crazy. She has her own opinion about my whole life and that leads me with the thought of will she always have this much control of me or will I break it. I found in history most only boys tend to not go that far from the nest but in my case I had plenty of plans and intentions to leave once I graduated but I felt as if no one was worried about me going to school and sure enough my mother, she did the least of them all and to think she does the most but do the least what I wanted to really ask her was why did you keep me around but when I do stick around you don't let me be who I want to be without your questions and commentary but most of all why did you never seem to help me when I wanted to leave so bad. I started to walk the train and when I got to the next car I was amazed to see it was a little boy sitting there to the right of me but it wasn't no little boy it was me and then he spoke and told me to take his hand and hold on tight. I think in my head o god not another one of these. Later a voice popped in my head and said be ready for 3 more because you ask the questions and now its time that you get your answers and we don't care the way you get them just as long as you get them. I begin to step forward and I go it feels like I'm /just floating in mid air all relaxed holding myself hand then all of a sudden we drop and land back at 465 Sylvia Rd. Apt k4 and he speaks and says look this is why should let you go and so how I phase the roof and I see my self in her arms and crying my eyes out and I couldn't help or stop the tears from falling. That was that Christmas day that my dad left me at the end of the side walk crying and my uncle can picked him up and drove off with me on the curb now crying as I begin to ball up the rain begins to fall and I start to think that its raining because I am crying but then I get back to crying and my mother is now running up and grabs me off the floor and runs me into the house and takes me upstairs and I just cant stop crying and I fall asleep crying and she kisses me on the forehead I begin to ascend up and I end up back on the roof and I ask him why did u bring me here and all I got was silence. Before I can run up and ask me again we flash forward and I start to turn around in a circle and realize this was the other day that she protected me it was the day that my aunt died and before I knew it I was in my old body I was that 6 year old boy again and then the bus stopped and the bus driver said ya'll can get off now and I get off the bus and my sister is walking with me and as we begin to descend down the hill my mother pulls up in the astro van and tell us to get in and we get down to the parking lot and we all get out and not know what to expect she turns to us and say she died today at 2 o'clock and I said who, who, who your aunt and all I felt was my heart drop and my knees get weak and I fell to the ground crying tears of sorrow and yelling no your lying she isn't and she rebuttals to me yes she is and I say its not fair why cant I go why cant I go with her why did she forget me behind its not fair. My legs regain there strength and I take off running for the apartment door and right as I started to run I got pulled out of the younger me and flew up to the roof again and he said do you see now why she wont let you go and I say with the tears still running down my face yes I'm her only boy and she don't want to see me fail or get hurt again I been through so much all she wants to do is to protect me but what she need to understand I can do it alone now I don't need here help anymore and before my eyes I well the me I was talking to ages and I can remember the sadness on my face and then I feel water rising and I said no but by now I know what's going on I come from under the water and I'm sitting in the bathroom tub crying my eyes out I had just tried to kill myself by drowning and then with the belt on the shower rod and all I can feel is the flash forward to all the random acts of my suicidal attempts that I made and I end up on the couch talking to my mother and crying telling her how I feel and I cant stand this and I don't want to be talked about and how that I felt like killing myself would solve everything cause I wont have to deal with this no more, and I said as I fell to mu knees in the living room still mommy im just to tired. She grabbed me once more off the floor and hugged me tightly and said I will protect you. Once again I am up on the roof top and saying stop I cant take it why are you taking me threw all of this I cant take it, then I replied you must endure prove to yourself that you belong in that world that this train is taking you back to, you said that this is your last trip here and me, you, we al want to not come back here anymore either. Can you give it all up and forget about it? No can you start over and try to become a new person? No because you become someone your not. I understand now why my mother says that she's ready for me to leave but when I do go to leave she really don't want me to; she don't want to see me crawl back to her and ask her to help me and save me or when I feel like its all to much, she wants me to stand my ground. I intend on doing so starting now, starting now. Before I can finish the last "NOW" I was back on train and was trying to figure out what just happened to me. I go to take a seat and I see coming down the aisle is a little blue boy in overalls and in a box hair cut with tears running down his face. I go up to him and say what's wrong and he looks up at me and I see its no ordinary boy, this, this is, I created you, your little boy blue. He said yes and he said hold on, I asked why and he said because of the next stop is a fall. By now we had started to go over the bridge but this bridge was no ordinary one either cause the train starts to lean forward and the tracks start to spiral, then the chairs disappear and I lunge forward and hit the glass and it begins to crack and it gives way and all I hear is glass shattering and falling but I hear a faint voice from a distance say network stream and it was like a portal opened up full of letter and numbers and four hands reached out and grabbed me and as I go threw I bump my head and black out. Awaking to four faces standing over me and saying is ok. I scream with terror and get up. I know you guys; each one of ya'll represent me as a toy Leona, Billy, Red Man and Batnet. You guys are supposed to be dead. Yes, we are al aware of that but where here to give you your next answer to your question Why you? No your not I don't want to hear this but you must for this is what u want and you shall get. In that same time they all merged together and it was boy blue and he asked me are you ready I replied no but I must they took me back to that day they day I stop believing in toys and magic and I stop trusting people and my faith but most, most of all my innocence was taking from me as I touched his hand I begin to feel the wind the happiness all around me; the feeing of being loved and liked but then it came time. That particular day me and my cousin was playing freeze tag and just basic tag and having fun until we started running around the house well in my aunt Mary case the two double wide trailers and as we begin to race I got behind them and then the back door of the 1st trailer opened and there stood 5'8 blonde hair black eyed albino women that asked me to help her move something out the house for her I said sure but let me go and get my cousins so we call can move it and it will be faster she quickly replied no I don't think that we need there help you will do just find I begin to walk up the stairs and go thru the house and as I made it almost to the kitchen she covered my mouth and whispered in my ear if you do anything I will kill you so I closed my mouth and she took me to the back room. There she started to take me clothes off and say you going to like this I will; the tears began to trickle down my face and she went to lift me then she said lay on the floor so I did. And for a whole hour she sucked me fucked me over and over and I the fact that I couldn't scream yell for help or do anything mad me more helpless and the hours came to a close she took me in the shower and she washed my body over and over I can still feel the lips kissing me on my cheek she took the one thing I had left my innocence and from that day on I wasn't no longer a child but a child in fear. She walked me to the door the back door and said you bet not say a word about what happen and for 14 years I didn't. As I was about to make it out the door blue pulled me out of the dream and said do you see why? No I don't see why me so blue replied it was you cause you was the strongest, it was you because you saved the others it was you because god said so but most of all it was you, its not right that we had to go thru that at all its not right that you felt that or still do feel that what is fair is that for your one sacrifice you saved three other ones from ever being touched. That day you were there angel. The water works came and he said the final thing and because of what happened you're a stronger person. I begin to float up and somehow I fall and hit my head and I awake and realize that I was just day dreaming or sleeping and I go back to try and to recall all of it and I cant and I would rather not go back to recall that horrifying dream.

I want to stay confined to my bed and think that everything will be ok but the truth is that it is going to be ok but in the back of my head the little tiny small voice is telling me that I just need to give it up I ask myself why should I give up now when I only reached part of my potential ant thinking that I can and will do better and be better than before. I once asked a question to facebook a question and it was when is it time to put up childish toys and get on my grown shit and the answer and no reply because I am the only one that tell me when its time. I've lost so much time and so many friends that I will not no wait I choose not to do it this time I got dreams and stuff that I want to do and I have to get to them now and stop putting my stuff on the back burner. I use to cry tears of sadness and now its nothing but tears of happiness. Telling the truth is said to always to be the truth but when I think of telling the truth I find it harder to do than others because I run it in my head and begin to think of the consciousness and the outcome rather then the big picture I look at the smaller picture and it how mad they will be in the mean time and it makes me think about one in particular myself.

So much can change and I still will end up as the same old person and in the same skin tired and worm out when can I shed my skin like a snake and get a new like I want to feel so much and yet once more I seem to be not ready still cooking so I say sit do my school work and be who I am to day waiting to see what is going to come up next I have so many plans and I wonder if love will be apart of that or does my solo rode ends.

She sat me down and told me that my guard is up and it its need to be down so I guess I can let it down.

I have started to come so far but I didn't get set back anyone I got set back because of me I did it I put my self back a step because what I thought that I was ready for something that I am not ready at all. On the outside I look like it but my inside still hasn't been fixed like I thought that it was fixed I'm in such a disarray and order inside that

I'm still hurting inside and waiting to be fixed but the one person that I thought could fix it isn't him or here its me its time that I put myself in the spotlight and take what I want and feel like it need it

To my surprise I was stabbed in my back
Then she used my love against me
Later I was tricked for my goodies
I was pushed from a train, while moving
I ended up in a town in the middle of nowhere
I can accustoms the strange but relaxed ways of life
I didn't want to go back to stay
So I went for a visit
Not too long just to see if I'm missed
To my surprise I wasn't so I left vowing never to return
I left my entire self there and started over
Now its two years later and she fixed me up
Stitched the heart up
Closed the open wound in the back
And gave me real love and came to visit and I went to visit to
She told me she missed me
Asked where I been and don't I think its time to come back
No answer I gave her but silence
I just knew she would leave now and never come back
But instead she stayed in contact
Via email, texting, and calling but most of all coming to see me
So I saved up the money and quit my job and went back to school
There I met her this particular girl game from
my past and showed and told me
You was missed and still is but asked
What happened this isn't the you I remember?
Life and a long vacation where I got comfortable with this
Then what was said to me by both girls
Get your ass up and get from under that
rock and out of your comfort zone
Cause bitch your throne is missing you and we are to
So now that I got the speeches

The bags are packed, the ticket is hand
And next stop home, to reclaim my throne
And to tell the world that this bitch is coming back
So get ready coming back with a pow and now
Jasmine and Princess my sweet girls your buddy is on his way in time

The semester is at a midpoint and I can say so far I manage to find myself getting closer to who I was and I start to forget and the new me starts to finally fade out and I can start to see that rode that got paved over with the black tar and the gravel. It starts to chip and crack and the bright light starts to shine threw and I see the gold rode that I need to be on and walking with no distractions in place. I walk with a shield and everything that comes toward me that isn't for me bounces back and I keep my head on straight and I don't get knocked out to walk down a detour once more. The funny thing that I have at least two more detours that I must go down and I know I am not ready and shouldn't be ready for a detour because it's not meant to be ready for they are meant to catch you off guard. These last two is about to do just that ugh!

Yet the truth is that I'm not ready to deal with the problem at hand or problems for that matter because my life that is the black hole has finally swallowed me up and left me her lying on the floor pill bottle in hand and crying tears of freedom because for once I am taking control of my life by finally ending this train wreck of a life by ....

Motherless Child:

I'm right here
Over here
No not over there
Right here look
Cant she hear me
I know she can see me
Wait, wait let me
Turn on the light
Ok now lets try again
Im right here look
Ok this isn't funny
Why isn't she acting
Like I don't exist
Why is she crying
Who is that in my bed
She calling my name
But she cant hear me
Im standing and now sitting
She still cant see me
Why is some many people me
And they all in black
I stop and freeze and the room begins to spin
And I figure out why
Its too late
Cause im already gone
Now six feet under
With the bugs and dirt
I ask why am I still here on earth and not up there
A voice replied "you left before you can feel something"
And it was a mothers love
And now Im dead and gone
Standing here transparent
And Still a motherless child
I fall to me knees in my corner and fade away
What I do best
Not existing to here

EXIST:

I ask myself
Do I exist or am I just there?
I've come so far but yet its still a challenge
My shoes are all worn and torn
My feet hurts from running so much
My eyes burn because I've cried so much
The thoughts, they try to come back over and over
And I call but this time no one answered
No one hears me no one can see the silent tears
No one can hear my the inner my crying out
Screaming to the top of my lungs asking
Begging, pleading for help
But no one comes
I go and run in to the room
That room
Another room trying to escaped
Get away and yet it keeps coming for me
It never ends
It tells me that I can get out
I don't have to feel like this
I don't have to live like this
But most of all it hears me
My cry for help
And its just one thing after this is all said and done
That I wont be heard no more at all
Cause the number 6 will go in to place and the
Dark is what I will only know
Silence stiff
Without life inside of me I lay
Content relaxed un heard but finally heard
And all it took was for me to take my own life
And to be lowered six feet under
And now they sit and cry
Scream hoop and holler
But for what you never heard me crying for help

So stop crying and deal like I did not being heard
So I Took a knife the sharpest one I can find went into the bathroom
Turned the light out
Fell to the floor
Cried silently in the bathroom thinking is this the best move
And I hold the knife in my right hand
And I jab it in my chest with my last bit of life
All I could do is cry
Because they didn't ever know

One Wish:

If I had one wish
And the thoughts came rushing in
One by one
With each and everyone having importance
Each demanding to be wished
But I
I, said I have one
Just one wish
That I think would change
My life back to normal
And the abuse
Yet verbal
And physical abuse
would go away
The breakdowns with tears
Tears that I cry is simply
Black as the tar pits dinosaurs died in it
The pain when they run down my face
Burn like acid
But its funny I come back to that one wish
The wish to exist
To be love
To be cared for
To matter to you, to her
To my mother
I wish that they day I told you
About me and my sexuality
I wish that day would have never came
I wish that I wouldn't have told you
I wish that my secret would still be my secret
And no one else's
I wish that my wish would come true
But I open my eyes that it was just a wish
Within my fantasy that I escape to
And I cry a tear of black tar and acid that burns my face
Because I know that my wish will never come true.